# Remember
## the 5th of
# November

First published in 2007 by
Franklin Watts
338 Euston Road
London
NW1 3BH

Franklin Watts Australia
Level 17/207 Kent Street
Sydney
NSW 2000

Text © Mick Gowar 2007
Illustration © Mike Phillips 2007

A CIP catalogue record for this book is available
from the British Library.

ISBN 978 0 7496 7083 2 (hbk)
ISBN 978 0 7496 7414 4 (pbk)

**Series Editor:** Melanie Palmer
**Series Advisor:** Dr Barrie Wade
**Series Designer:** Peter Scoulding

Printed in China

Franklin Watts is a division of
Hachette Children's Books.

# HOPSCOTCH HISTORIES

# Remember
## the 5th of
# November

By Mick Gowar and Mike Phillips

# W
## FRANKLIN WATTS
### LONDON•SYDNEY

## About this book

Some of the characters in this book are made up,
but the subject is based on real events in history.
In 1605, a group of men plotted to kill the Protestant
King of England, James I, and blow up Parliament.
They wanted England to return to the Catholic religion.
On 4th November 1605, guards found a man in the
cellars under Parliament, hiding 36 barrels of gunpowder.
The man said his name was John Johnson but he later
confessed to being Guy Fawkes. Soon afterwards, the
rest of the plotters were caught and joined Guy in the
Tower of London. They were all tried and executed.

Once, I was a hero. I helped save
the King and Parliament from
being blown up. Here is my story ...

I was one of Lord Monteagle's servants. One night, I went to the inn to get some wine for my master's supper.

Some men were inside, whispering:

"Guy – you guard the gunpowder.

On the 5th, you light the fuse and – "

They stopped when they saw me.

I bought the wine and left.
One of the men from the inn
followed me outside.

"Take this letter to Lord Monteagle,
and hurry!" he said. Then he
disappeared into the dark.

I ran back as fast as I could and gave my master the letter.

Master looked shocked. He stopped eating and got up.

If you want to live, stay away from the opening of Parliament. They will receive a terrible blow!

"We must show this letter to Lord
Salisbury at once," said my master.

14

We rode to Lord Salisbury's house
as fast as we could.

Lord Salisbury read the letter.
"There's a plot to cause trouble
at the opening of Parliament,"
he said.

"The King is in danger! Take these men. Search Parliament and all the houses nearby."

Master and I rode through the dark
streets of London to Parliament
with the King's guards.

"Some men have rented that house.
Its cellars go right underneath
Parliament," a woman told us.

"Search the cellars!" said the Captain of the guards. My master and I followed them inside.

A man was in the cellars.

"Who are you? What are you

doing?" asked the Captain.

"I'm John Johnson," said the man.
"I'm just getting firewood ready
for the winter."

"He's lying!" I said. "I've seen
that man before. He was at the
inn the night I was given the
letter. His name is Guy."

"Search behind those logs!" ordered the Captain. We found 36 barrels of gunpowder. It was enough to blow up everyone in Parliament!

"Seize him!" ordered the Captain.
"Take him to the King!"

Guy was taken to the King's bed
chamber. The King was woken up.
"This man plotted to kill you!"
said the Captain.

"Take him to the Tower!"
commanded the King. "We will
know everything, and those to
blame will be punished."

So when you light bonfires and sing your song: **Remember, remember the 5th of November, Gunpowder, treason and plot ...**

Remember me too, and how I helped to save the King's life.

Hopscotch has been specially designed to fit the requirements of the National Literacy Strategy. It offers real books by top authors and illustrators for children developing their reading skills. There are 49 Hopscotch stories to choose from:

**Marvin, the Blue Pig**
ISBN 978 0 7496 4619 6

**Plip and Plop**
ISBN 978 0 7496 4620 2

**The Queen's Dragon**
ISBN 978 0 7496 4618 9

**Flora McQuack**
ISBN 978 0 7496 4621 9

**Willie the Whale**
ISBN 978 0 7496 4623 3

**Naughty Nancy**
ISBN 978 0 7496 4622 6

**Run!**
ISBN 978 0 7496 4705 6

**The Playground Snake**
ISBN 978 0 7496 4706 3

**"Sausages!"**
ISBN 978 0 7496 4707 0

**The Truth about Hansel and Gretel**
ISBN 978 0 7496 4708 7

**Pippin's Big Jump**
ISBN 978 0 7496 4710 0

**Whose Birthday Is It?**
ISBN 978 0 7496 4709 4

**The Princess and the Frog**
ISBN 978 0 7496 5129 9

**Flynn Flies High**
ISBN 978 0 7496 5130 5

**Clever Cat**
ISBN 978 0 7496 5131 2

**Moo!**
ISBN 978 0 7496 5332 3

**Izzie's Idea**
ISBN 978 0 7496 5334 7

**Roly-poly Rice Ball**
ISBN 978 0 7496 5333 0

**I Can't Stand It!**
ISBN 978 0 7496 5765 9

**Cockerel's Big Egg**
ISBN 978 0 7496 5767 3

**How to Teach a Dragon Manners**
ISBN 978 0 7496 5873 1

**The Truth about those Billy Goats**
ISBN 978 0 7496 5766 6

**Marlowe's Mum and the Tree House**
ISBN 978 0 7496 5874 8

**Bear in Town**
ISBN 978 0 7496 5875 5

**The Best Den Ever**
ISBN 978 0 7496 5876 2

## ADVENTURE STORIES

**Aladdin and the Lamp**
ISBN 978 0 7496 6692 7

**Blackbeard the Pirate**
ISBN 978 0 7496 6690 3

**George and the Dragon**
ISBN 978 0 7496 6691 0

**Jack the Giant-Killer**
ISBN 978 0 7496 6693 4

## TALES OF KING ARTHUR

**1. The Sword in the Stone**
ISBN 978 0 7496 6694 1

**2. Arthur the King**
ISBN 978 0 7496 6695 8

**3. The Round Table**
ISBN 978 0 7496 6697 2

**4. Sir Lancelot and the Ice Castle**
ISBN 978 0 7496 6698 9

## TALES OF ROBIN HOOD

**Robin and the Knight**
ISBN 978 0 7496 6699 6

**Robin and the Monk**
ISBN 978 0 7496 6700 9

**Robin and the Friar**
ISBN 978 0 7496 6702 3

**Robin and the Silver Arrow**
ISBN 978 0 7496 6703 0

## FAIRY TALES

**The Emperor's New Clothes**
ISBN 978 0 7496 7077 1 *
ISBN 978 0 7496 7421 2

**Cinderella**
ISBN 978 0 7496 7073 3 *
ISBN 978 0 7496 7417 5

**Snow White**
ISBN 978 0 7496 7074 0 *
ISBN 978 0 7496 7418 2

**Jack and the Beanstalk**
ISBN 978 0 7496 7078 8 *
ISBN 978 0 7496 7422 9

**The Three Billy Goats Gruff**
ISBN 978 0 7496 7076 4 *
ISBN 978 0 7496 7420 5

**The Pied Piper of Hamelin**
ISBN 978 0 7496 7075 7 *
ISBN 978 0 7496 7419 9

## HISTORIES

**Toby and the Great Fire of London**
ISBN 978 0 7496 7079 5 *
ISBN 978 0 7496 7410 6

**Pocahontas the Peacemaker**
ISBN 978 0 7496 7080 1 *
ISBN 978 0 7496 7411 3

**Grandma's Seaside Bloomers**
ISBN 978 0 7496 7081 8 *
ISBN 978 0 7496 7412 0

**Hoorah for Mary Seacole**
ISBN 978 0 7496 7082 5 *
ISBN 978 0 7496 7413 7

**Remember the 5th of November**
ISBN 978 0 7496 7083 2 *
ISBN 978 0 7496 7414 4

**Tutankhamun and the Golden Chariot**
ISBN 978 0 7496 7084 9 *
ISBN 978 0 7496 7415 1

* hardback